What Do You Know!

Lorinda Bryan Cauley

G. P. Putnam's Sons • New York

For my daughter,
Erin,
with love

Here's a game.
Come on, let's go!
Join right in—
show what you know!

Ape starts with A,
Bug starts with B.

Look for the things
that start with C.

Cat rhymes with Rat,
Bear rhymes with Hare.

Think of the words
that rhyme with Mare.

Point to a circle,
point to a square.

Point to the apple,
point to the pear.

Red mixed with white
makes the color pink.

Two colors make green.
Which ones do you think?

Spy something purple,
spy something blue.

Spy something yellow,
and something orange too.

Count to five,
then count to ten.

Now count to twenty
and back again!

Count all the insects
that you can see . . .

flying in the air
and all around the tree.

Which animal says "quack"?
Which one says "moo"?

Which animal has feathers
and says "cock-a-doodle-doo"?

Monkeys eat bananas.
Crocodiles eat meat.

What's bunny rabbit's favorite thing to eat?

The opposite of up
is all the way down.

What do you think
is the opposite of frown?

Pairs are things
that come in twos.

Find all the pairs
besides my shoes!

A teacup, a pencil,
a key and a mitten.

Look very closely.
Where are they hidden?

Here's another
fun little game.

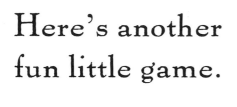

Point to the things
that are the same.

Look on this page.
Some things are wrong.

Find seven things
that don't belong.

It was fun to play.
Now it's time to go.
It's terrific
how much you know!